This book belongs to…

For my patients at the MassGeneral Hospital *for* Children with gratitude
for all that they have taught and given me. —C.C.

For Michael, who makes it all possible. —F.S.B.

Other Dr. Hippo Stories

The Little Elephant with the Big Earache

Katie Caught a Cold

Upcoming books from The Hippocratic Press

Look for Dr. Hippo in upcoming stories: A giraffe with a sore throat
and a moose with loose poops are coming soon!

Ordering information

Order books from your local book retailer, your online book source, or directly from:

The Hippocratic Press

281A Fairhaven Hill Road

Concord, MA 01742

www.hippocraticpress.com

Library of Congress Control Number: 2005926039

ISBN 0-9753516-2-1

THE HIPPOCRATIC PRESS · CONCORD, MASSACHUSETTS

Peeper Has a Fever

by Charlotte Cowan, M.D.   illustrated by Susan Banta

book design by Labor Day Creative

THE HIPPOCRATIC PRESS
CONCORD, MA

Peeper woke up with a start.

"Today's the Picnic, Lily!" he exclaimed, hopping out of bed.

"Mom," began Peeper,
"the Picnic and Diving
Contest are today!"

"I know, Peeper,"
smiled his mother.
"Come have breakfast."

Peeper sat down.
"Yum, pancakes!"
he said.

But he hardly touched his food.

"Peeper, eat up," encouraged his Mom.

"I'm not hungry," he said. "Hopper's outside. I'm going, too."

"Peeper, Peeper, I found you!" laughed Lily.

"You're not allowed out here," said Peeper. "You'll fall in
and get eaten up by a big fish! Come on, Lilypad, let's go inside."

His Mom gasped. "Peeper, are you all right? You're flushed—and feel so hot!"

"Oh sweet pea, I bet
you have a fever."

"I'm fine, Mom,"
said Peeper. "I *can't*
be sick today!"

"Peeper, even if you're sick, maybe we can go to the Picnic today and see Dr. Hippocrates tomorrow."

His mother read the thermometer: "104°! Oh, Peeps! I'm calling the doctor. Are you really okay?"

"I just feel cold, Mom, that's all."

Peeper pulled up his covers and listened: "Hello, Dr. Hippo? I'm worried about my Peeper. He is 104° Fahrenheit—or 40° Centigrade!"

Peeper imagined Dr. Hippo talking.
He always said:

- "How's my favorite pollywog?"
- "Goodness, how you've
  grown, my friend!"
- "Happy hopping, Peeper!"

Peeper smiled.

His Mom continued, "I see: The fever's
the *beginning* of an infection. Other
symptoms may appear soon—like a
runny nose or a rash. Yes, I'll call
back tomorrow for sure, or later
today if Peeper looks worse.
Thanks, Dr. Hippo!"

Peeper sighed. "I'm *not* sick. I'm *fine*, but you're bugging me, Lily. Buzz off."

Peeper fell asleep.

He woke up to the sound of voices. "No Picnic for Peeper," said his Mom. "He might get his friends sick."

"Poor Peeps!" replied his Dad. "What's causing his fever?"

"Dr. Hippo said it's too soon to tell. We just need to wait—and to keep Peeper comfortable."

"I'll take care of Peeps," offered his Dad.

Peeper couldn't believe his ears.
"Not go to the picnic? *No way!*"

He got out of bed—but couldn't
hop. "Mom," he complained, "I
hurt all over and I'm *so* cold!"

"Come on, sweet Peeps," she said.
"Your fever's playing tricks on you:
It makes you feel cold but you're
really too hot!"

"This medicine will help you feel better, Peeper. It'll take away your aches and chills. Would you like some ice cream afterwards?"

"Yes, please," said Peeper.

"Sweet pea," added his Mom, "I know it's confusing, but cooling you off will help, too. We'll start with a bath."

"Is the water okay, Peeps?" asked his Dad.

"It's raining on my boat," said Peeper.

His father smiled. "Dr. Hippo said to keep you *'cool and out of school.'* We can do that. And we'll fix up the *Firefly*, too."

"Okay, Dad," said Peeper. "Just let me finish my sprinkling first."

"We're going to the Picnic with the Speckles," announced Peeper's Mom. "I'm so sorry you can't come, Peeps, but I made you a smoothie."

"Thanks, Mom. I wish I could come, too," said Peeper.

Soon the Speckles paddled up in their canoe. "Welcome aboard, Lily," they said. "Good-bye, Peeper!"

"Good-bye," he replied. He added quietly, "It's not fair. I hope Lily falls in and gets eaten up by a *giant* fish!"

Peeper put his head down.

Before long, he heard his Dad
calling: "Peeper, I need you.
Out here. I'm painting the *Firefly*."

Peeper left the kitchen. "Hey, this medicine must *work*," he thought. "I can hop again!"

He yelled, "Coming, Dad!"

"Grab a brush, and help me paint the bottom," invited his Dad.

Peeper found a paintbrush and joined him. "How soon can we sail the *Firefly* again?"

"Maybe tomorrow... Oh no, is that rain?"

They went inside when
the rain came.

"It's time for a nap
anyway, Peeps," said
his Dad. "I'll be in the
kitchen making dinner."

"The Picnic was such fun," exclaimed Peeper's Mom, "but the Diving Contest was postponed until Saturday. Maybe Peeper can dive after all!"

"And," added Lily, "we got him a surprise!"

When Peeper woke up, the
family had dinner together.
"I'm not hungry," he said.

"Have a popsicle instead, Peeps,"
urged his mother.

"Thanks, Mom, and thanks for
the balloons!"

Lily beamed: "I told you he'd like them!"

After dinner, his Dad
asked, "Would you like
a story, Peeps?"

"*Three* stories, please,"
smiled Peeper.

His mother tucked Peeper into
bed. "Good night, sweet
Peeps," she said. "Great job
taking your medicine
today. Sleep well,
and make sure Sal
sleeps well, too."

"He'll be fine,
Mom. Good
night."

Peeper's fever lasted for a few days and then, one morning, something funny happened.

"Mom!" Peeper shouted, "I'm all spotted—just like Sal!"

His mother smiled: "Dr. Hippo thought you might get a rash, Peeps. You'll be okay: It'll go away soon, and so will your fever."

Peeper was all better by Saturday when he and his father set off for the Diving Contest.

"Maybe I'll win a ribbon, Mom!" shouted Peeper.

"Of course you will," she cheered. "You're *Hot Stuff*, Peeps!